Welcome to ALADDIN QUIX!

If you are looking for fast, fun-to-read stories with colorful characters, lots of kid-friendly humor, easy-to-follow action, entertaining story lines, and lively illustrations, then **ALADDIN QUIX** is for you!

But wait, there's more!

If you're also looking for stories with tables of contents; word lists; about-the-book questions; 64, 80, or 96 pages; short chapters; short paragraphs; and large fonts, then **ALADDIN QUIX** is *definitely* for you!

ALADDIN QUIX: The next step between ready to reads and longer, more challenging chapter books, for readers five to eight years old.

**Read all the books in the
Royal Sweets series!**

Book 1: *A Royal Rescue*
Book 2: *Sugar Secrets*
Book 3: *Stolen Jewels*
Book 4: *The Marshmallow Ghost*
Book 5: *Chocolate Challenge*

ROYAL SWEETS

Chocolate Challenge

By Helen Perelman

Illustrated by Olivia Chin Mueller

ALADDIN QUIX

New York London Toronto Sydney New Delhi

For Captain Nathan —H. P.

ALADDIN QUIX
Simon & Schuster Children's Publishing Division
1230 Avenue of the Americas, New York, New York 10020
First Aladdin QUIX paperback edition August 2020
Text copyright © 2020 by Helen Perelman
Illustrations copyright © 2020 by Olivia Chin Mueller
Also available in an Aladdin QUIX hardcover edition.
All rights reserved, including the right of reproduction in whole or in part in any form.
ALADDIN and the related marks and colophon are trademarks of Simon & Schuster, Inc.
For information about special discounts for bulk purchases, please contact Simon & Schuster
Special Sales at 1-866-506-1949 or business@simonandschuster.com.
The Simon & Schuster Speakers Bureau can bring authors to your live event. For more information
or to book an event contact the Simon & Schuster Speakers Bureau at 1-866-248-3049
or visit our website at www.simonspeakers.com.
Series designed by Jessica Handelman
Book designed by Tiara Iandiorio
The illustrations for this book were rendered digitally.
The text of this book was set in Archer Medium.
Manufactured in the United States of America 0720 OFF
2 4 6 8 10 9 7 5 3 1
Names: Perelman, Helen, author. | Mueller, Olivia Chin, illustrator. | Perelman, Helen. Royal sweets ; 5.
Title: Chocolate challenge / by Helen Perelman ; illustrated by Olivia Chin Mueller.
Description: [First edition] | New York : Aladdin QUIX, 2020. | Series: Royal sweets ; 5 |
Audience: Ages 5-8. | Summary: Princess Mini takes the chocolates she has made to her friend,
Gobo the troll, and he takes her on an exciting, dangerous, and messy boat ride down the Chocolate
River—and she encourages him to enter the beginners race at the Chocolate River Run.
Identifiers: LCCN 2020009784 (print) | LCCN 2020009785 (eBook) |
ISBN 9781534455061 (hardcover) | ISBN 9781534455054 (paperback) | ISBN 9781534455078 (eBook)
Subjects: LCSH: Fairies—Juvenile fiction. | Trolls—Juvenile fiction. | Princesses—Juvenile fiction. |
Chocolate—Juvenile fiction. | Friendship—Juvenile fiction. | Boats and boating—Juvenile fiction. |
Racing—Juvenile fiction. | CYAC: Fairies—Fiction. | Trolls—Fiction. | Princesses—Fiction. |
Chocolate—Fiction. | Friendship—Fiction. | Boats and boating—Fiction. | Racing—Fiction.
Classification: LCC PZ7.P42488 Cg 2020 (print) | LCC PZ7.P42488 (eBook) | DDC 813.6 [Fic]—dc23
LC record available at https://lccn.loc.gov/2020009784
LC eBook record available at https://lccn.loc.gov/2020009785

Cast of Characters

Princess Mini: Royal fairy princess of Candy Kingdom

Sir Nougat: Teacher at Royal Fairy Academy

Princess Taffy: Princess Mini's best friend

Prince Frosting: One of Princess Mini's cousins from Cake Kingdom

Lady Cherry: Teacher at Royal Fairy Academy

Gobo: Troll living in Sugar Valley

Princess Cupcake: Prince Frosting's twin

Princess Swirlie: Princess Cupcake's best friend

Butterscotch: Princess Mini's royal unicorn

Beanie: Royal chef

Princess Lolli: Princess Mini's mother and ruling fairy princess of Candy Kingdom

Toomie: Gobo's older brother

Contents

1

Choc-o-rific Playdate

"Princess Mini," **Sir Nougat** said. "Your chocolate squares look perfect. Well done!"

"Thank you," I said to my teacher. Sir Nougat was teaching the first-year students at Royal Fairy

Academy how to decorate chocolate. **Princess Taffy**, my best friend, used taffy pieces. **Prince Frosting**, my cousin, put icing all over his pieces. And I carefully lined white mini chocolate chips on my chocolates.

"Students," Sir Nougat said, clapping his hands. "Please finish up."

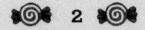

Lady Cherry, our classroom teacher, flew into the room. She smiled as she looked around at our chocolates. "Nice work," she said to the class. "After you clean your area, please line up for **dismissal**."

I turned to Taffy. "I am going to bring these chocolates to **Gobo**'s house today."

"You have a playdate at Gobo's house?" **Princess Cupcake** asked. Cupcake was Frosting's twin, but she was much more sour and sometimes mean.

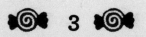 3

"Yes!" I said. I tried to ignore her look of surprise.

Gobo was a troll who lived in Sugar Valley. I met him on the first day of school and helped him out of a sticky situation. **He got stuck in a caramel bush!** After that day, we became fast friends.

Princess Swirlie, Cupcake's best friend, came over to me. She wrinkled up her nose. "I have never been to a troll's house."

"Me neither!" Cupcake

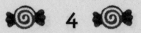

exclaimed. "Imagine a playdate *not* at a castle!"

Cupcake and Swirlie flew to the door. Taffy leaned over. "Don't pay attention to them," she said.

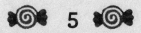

"I know," I said. "I am excited to go to Gobo's house." I wrapped up my chocolate squares and put them in my basket. "My mom spoke to his mom and the plan is set."

"You're lucky," Frosting told me. "It's not every day a Candy Fairy gets to visit a troll's house."

"That's for sure," Taffy said. "I bet you will have a really good time."

"Thanks," I said, smiling at my friends. I patted my basket. "Do

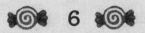

you think his family will like these chocolates?"

"They look **sugar-tastic**!" Taffy exclaimed. "They will love them!"

The final bell of the day rang. Lady Cherry dismissed our class. Outside in the courtyard, my unicorn, **Butterscotch**, was waiting for me. She is the best royal unicorn. I said goodbye to my friends and climbed up onto Butterscotch's back.

When I arrived home, **Beanie**

was waiting for me in the castle kitchen. She is the royal chef and makes the best after-school snacks. I showed her my chocolates.

"Well done," Beanie said. "You are doing very well at school, Princess Mini."

She gave me an extra fruit roll.

My mom, **Princess Lolli**, flew into the kitchen. She is the ruling fairy princess in Candy Kingdom. I showed her what I made in class.

"Oh, sweet sugars," she said. "You are learning so much

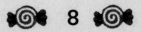

at Royal Fairy Academy. These chocolates are perfect!"

"I am going to give these to Gobo," I said. "I want to give his family a chocolate surprise." I put the chocolates in a box and tied red licorice rope around the middle. "How does this look?"

"Delicious!" Beanie exclaimed. She flew over to the counter by the door. "A sugar fly dropped this letter off for you." She handed me a tiny envelope.

"It's from Gobo!" I said.

Sugar flies were so helpful and flew messages to fairies and trolls around Candy Kingdom. I hoped nothing was wrong.

I quickly read Gobo's letter. He wrote that I should meet him in Peppermint Grove instead of at his house. **"I have a surprise for you!"** he wrote.

I showed the letter to my mom.

"It looks like you *both* have surprises," she said. "Butterscotch will take you once you are ready."

I wondered what Gobo's sur-

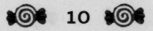

prise would be. **Sure as sugar,**
we were going to have a super
choc-o-rific playdate!

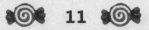

2

Sweet Sailing

Butterscotch's wide purple wings beat up and down as we moved quickly through the kingdom. High in the sky, I spotted Chocolate River. The river twisted through the middle of Candy Kingdom.

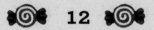

I held the box of the chocolates I made in my hands.

Butterscotch landed on the soft sugar sands near the river in Peppermint Grove. "Thank you for the ride, Butterscotch," I said. I flew off her back. "This is where Gobo said to meet," I added.

Only, I didn't see Gobo anywhere. **"Hello?"** I called. **"Gobo?"**

I looked over at Butterscotch. Her ears were raised. She seemed a little nervous too.

"The sugar fly message said to

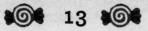

meet here," I said to Butterscotch. "We are right on time." I scratched my head.

Butterscotch **swooshed** her tail and looked left and right. Her ears were straight up, listening for clues.

"**Gobo?**" I called again. I flew up above the trees. I saw peppermint bushes and lots of candy canes, but not Gobo. I flew back down to Butterscotch.

Just then I heard, "**Princess Mini!**"

It was Gobo.

I spun around. I didn't see him.

"Where are you?" I yelled. "Are you stuck again?"

"**Look over here!**" Gobo answered.

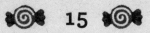

Butterscotch moved closer to Chocolate River. We stood on the sand and looked out into the rushing water.

Gobo was on a boat!

"Wow!" I exclaimed.

"Are you surprised?" Gobo asked. He sailed the boat to the shore.

"Yes!" I said.

Gobo jumped out onto the sand, pulled the boat closer, and tied it to a nearby tree.

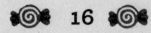

"When did you get a boat?" I asked, smiling.

Gobo stood proudly. "I built this with my dad," he said.

"Gobo, this is **sugar-tastic**!" I told him. "You must have worked really hard."

"Stitching the sail was the hardest part," Gobo said. He looked up at the large sail. "We had to sew the fruit leather together, and that was pretty sticky."

"This sure is a surprise!" I cried.

"The boat's name is *Mint Magic*," Gobo said. He pointed to the back of the boat where the name was written in black letters. "We hung extra mints on the sides

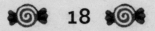

of the boat and got the largest candy cane for the **mast**."

"Choc-o-rific!" I said. "This is the nicest boat I have ever seen."

Gobo blushed. "Thank you," he said. Then he looked up at me. "Do you want a ride to my house?"

I didn't know what to say. I had never been on a boat before.

"Don't be scared," Gobo said.

"You knew I was scared?" I asked. "How did you know?"

Gobo laughed. "Your wings

 19

flutter very fast when you are nervous," he said.

My wings *were* moving fast. I didn't realize I was off the ground! "I'm used to being in the air, not on the water," I told him.

Gobo puffed out his chest. "I am a really good sailor," he said. "Come aboard!"

I told Butterscotch to meet me later at Gobo's house. She nodded her head and then flapped her wings to lift off. I flew onto the boat.

"Have a seat," Gobo instructed

me. "Stay here in the middle." He pointed to the fruit-leather straps on the side of the boat. "And hold on here."

"I'm ready," I said. I held on very tightly. The box of chocolates was in my lap.

Gobo pushed the boat off the sand.

The boat rocked back and forth in the water. I looked up and saw the sail puff out from a **gust** of wind. Gobo held the rope tight, and we moved down the river.

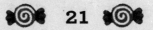

"And away we go!"

Gobo said.

I held on to the strap—and held my breath!

3

Strong Winds

The wind filled the sail and blew my hair back. I stretched out my legs and took a deep breath. The water made swishing sounds against the boat, and I started to enjoy the ride.

"Sailing is fun," I said, grinning at Gobo.

"I'm glad you like the ride," Gobo said.

"How long did this take you to build?" I asked.

"My dad and I worked together for months. He built a boat with his dad when he was young. He also built one with **Toomie**, my older brother. Toomie races his boat. He named it *Fast Flyer*!"

"Are you going to race your boat?" I asked.

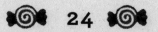

Gobo shrugged. "Maybe," he said. He looked down at the water. "Toomie is the racer in the family."

"Why can't there be *two* racers in a family?" I asked.

Gobo let the sail out a little. We moved faster. "Toomie has lots of **trophies**," he said.

"Maybe you will win some trophies," I said. I watched Gobo's face. "Do you want to race?"

Gobo slowly nodded his head. "I think I would like to," he said.

"There is a race next week. But I'm not sure."

I remembered hearing about the Chocolate River Race at the castle. **"Gobo! You should enter!"** I said.

Gobo shifted the rope in his hand. "I'm not sure," he said. "What if I don't get a trophy?"

"Maybe you won't win this race," I said. "But maybe you will. **You have to try."**

"I guess," Gobo said. He looked up. The wind was rippling the sail,

so he pulled the rope tighter. "For now, maybe I should just sail with friends," he said.

"I'm happy to sail with you," I replied.

Gobo blushed. "Actually, Mini, you are my first passenger," he said.

"I am very honored," I answered.

I looked around at the shore. The view of Chocolate Woods from a boat was different from the sky. "You can see anything from the boat that you can't see

 27

when flying above the woods," I told Gobo. "I didn't know so many chocolate flowers grew on the shore."

Gobo steered the boat closer to the flowers.

"The flowers are delicious," Gobo said. He leaned over and plucked two for us.

Gobo was right. The flower was yummy. As I ate, I looked down at the water. A few gummy fish were swimming alongside the boat. They were red, green,

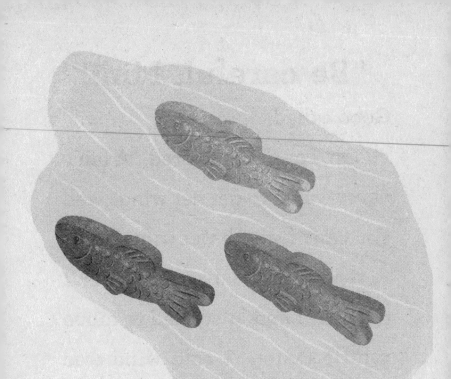

and yellow. **I had never seen so many!** "I didn't realize how many fish there are in the river," I said. I leaned over to get a better view.

"Be careful, Mini!"

Gobo called.

"Oh, I am," I answered. "A fairy *never* wants to get her wings wet. You can't fly with wet wings!"

When the boat sailed around the next bend, it started to move a little faster. A cold wind was blowing, and the branches on the trees swayed back and forth.

"Grab the straps!" Gobo called.

Large black clouds filled the sky, and the daylight **vanished**.

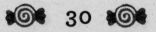

"Oh no!" I cried. **"There is a storm blowing in!"**

"Hold on!" Gobo yelled.

The sail on the boat was flapping in the strong wind.

Gobo pulled the rope hard, tightening the sail. Suddenly, it felt as if we were in a race!

"My wings!" I cried. "They're going to get wet!"

Gobo threw me a blanket he had on the boat. I wrapped it around my shoulders to protect my wings before the rain started.

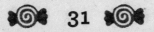

31

I tried hard not to flutter them. I scrunched down low and held on to the gift for Gobo's family.

"Don't worry," Gobo yelled. "This storm will move quickly."

"This storm came out of nowhere!" I yelled back.

The gusts pushed the sail, and the boat sailed **faster and faster** down the river. If we were in a race, we would definitely win! I could barely breathe!

Gobo didn't let go of the rope once. He didn't seem scared at all,

even though the wind continued.

I closed my eyes and pulled the blanket over my head. I hoped the storm would end soon.

4

Chocolate Mess

After a couple minutes, it felt like the wind and the boat *finally* slowed down. I lifted the blanket off my head and opened my eyes. "Did the storm pass?"

"Yes," Gobo said. "Are you okay?"

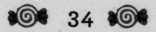

"I was so scared!" I said. I kept the blanket wrapped around me.

"Me too," Gobo admitted.

"You didn't seem scared," I said. "You were very brave."

Gobo stood on the edge of the boat. He was still **gripping** the rope, but he relaxed a little now that the wind wasn't blasting.

I looked down at the box in my lap. It was dripping with melted chocolate!

"My surprise is ruined!" I said. "I made special chocolates

 35

for your family, and now they're all messy and melted. I must have squeezed the box too tightly when I was under the blanket!"

"Oh no!" Gobo said. He handed me a cloth to wipe my hands.

"What a mess!" I said.

"I like messes," Gobo said. "Especially if they are made of chocolate!"

I shook my head. "I wanted to bring your family a special treat," I said. "I just learned how to decorate these chocolates." I looked down at the box of melted chocolate. "This is not the gift I wanted to give."

"Wait," Gobo said. He snapped his fingers. **"I have an idea!"**

"You do?" I asked.

"You can make a *different* kind of

candy," he said. "Let me show you."

The boat moved along the river, and Gobo slowed down at the edge of Chocolate Woods.

"Over there," he said, pointing. "Do you see that caramel bush?"

"Is that the bush that you got stuck in?" I asked.

Gobo laughed. **"Yes!"** he said. "This is the spot where we first met. Remember how I couldn't move?" He rubbed his backside and smiled. "I was so happy to see you that day! You helped me

out of a very sticky situation."

Gobo tossed the rope out to a tree stump and pulled the boat to shore. "Now I can help *you* out of a gooey situation!" He jumped off and pulled a caramel off the bush.

"We can dip these in the melted chocolate," Gobo said.

"That is a **choc-o-rific** idea!" I exclaimed.

"Let's try it out," Gobo said.

I opened the box. Gobo dipped a caramel into the chocolate and set it down on a large chocolate banana leaf.

"Maybe we should try one," I said, popping it into my mouth. **"Mmmm!"** The caramel and chocolate tasted delicious together.

Gobo had one too. **"Yum,"** he said, smiling. "I love these! Let's make more."

One by one we dipped the caramels into the chocolate. I found another chocolate banana leaf and folded the tiny chocolates inside. I took some gummy flowers from the riverbank and tied them in the middle.

"This looks much better now," I said. "Thank you, Gobo."

"And they taste good, too!" he said, licking his fingers.

We returned to the boat. I sat in the middle, and Gobo stood at the front.

I watched him set the sail and head back out on the water.

"You *really* should race this weekend," I said. "You knew just what to do when the wind was blowing hard. You are ready."

"Maybe," Gobo said.

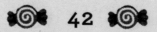

When Gobo didn't answer right away, I thought I had a chance to **convince** him. He should race his *Mint Magic*!

5

Fair Trade

Large purple rocks lined the edge of Chocolate Woods. I knew Gobo lived there, but I had never been inside the caves. I walked with him through a long rocky tunnel. At the end I saw his front door,

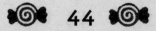

which was made of licorice logs. There was a large welcome mat in front of the doorway.

"This is **sugar-tastic**," I said.

Gobo opened the door. "Hello," he announced. **"I'm home!"**

His parents and Toomie were there to greet us. Gobo looked like a **combination** of his parents. He had his mom's eyes and his dad's

head shape. His brother, Toomie, was a little taller and had red hair, but he looked **similar** to Gobo.

"Welcome to our home!" his mom greeted me.

Gobo's father grinned at me and said, "This is the first time a Candy Fairy has come to visit."

I thought of what my mother might say. "I'm happy to be the first," I said, with a royal smile. "Thank you for inviting me."

I felt Toomie staring at my wings. I knew they were fluttering fast. I

took a deep breath and stayed put with my feet on the ground.

"Nice to meet you," Toomie said.

"Thank you," I said. "Nice to meet you, too." I walked over to Gobo's mother and handed her the gift.

She opened up the banana leaf. **"Chocolate caramels!"** she exclaimed. "One of our favorites. Thank you, Mini," she said.

I was very glad we had fixed my melted mess.

Gobo took my hand. "Come see my room," he said.

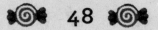

I followed Gobo down the hall. His room was a large square carved out of the purple rocks. His bed was in the far corner with a fluffy blue and white blanket. On the floor was a round yellow rug that matched

the color of a chair in the corner.

I spotted a row of color-
ful sugar marbles on the shelf
above the yellow chair. "You
collect sugar marbles too?" I
asked. **"And you put them
in rainbow order!"**

"Yes," Gobo replied. "You do too?"

I laughed. "I always have to fix
the order when I get a new one,"
I said. I looked at all of Gobo's
marbles. He didn't have many
blues. "I can trade you some blue
ones, if you want."

 50

"Really?" Gobo asked. "I have lots of red marbles to trade."

"Red marbles are hard for me to find," I said. I picked up one of the large ones. "Where do you find all these really big red ones?"

"I found those in the Sugar Caves," he said. "You have to know where to look." He took two red-colored marbles off his shelf. "Here are two reds, and you can bring me two blues tomorrow."

"A fair trade," I said. "Thank you!"

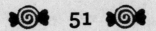

On Gobo's floor I spotted an invitation for the Chocolate River Race. I picked it up. I pointed to the schedule on the bottom of the page. There was a list of five races. "'A beginner race,'" I read.

"Gobo, this race is perfect for you!"

Gobo shrugged. "You think so?" he said. "I'm not sure."

"Did you ask your parents?" I asked.

Gobo nodded. "Yes, they want me to enter. Toomie is racing in the second race."

"Then you have to!" I said. "I can't wait to tell Taffy and Frosting."

"Maybe you shouldn't tell them," Gobo said. He sat down

on his bed. "I may come in last place."

I shook my head. "We will all be there. We don't care what place you come in. We're your friends! We will be there to cheer you on!"

6

Go, Gobo!

A few days later Taffy, Frosting, and I were making signs for the Chocolate River Race in my bedroom. I held up the sign I was working on.

"How is this?" I asked them.

"Gobo will love that!" Taffy exclaimed.

I had carefully glued choco- late sprinkles on the letters **G-O, G-O-B-O!**

I thought the sign looked pretty sweet. I hoped Gobo would like it.

"I have never been to the boat race," Frosting said.

"My mom told me there will be more boats entered than last year," I said. "She said this will be the biggest race ever."

Taffy glued a stick onto the back of her sign. "I am happy for Gobo," she said.

"This is a big day for him," I said.

"I hope he wins a trophy," Frosting added.

"Not everyone will," I said.

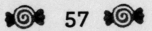

My parents called for us to come downstairs. We flew to the back courtyard and got on our unicorns to take us to Chocolate River. We wanted to get there early to find the best spot to watch the race.

There were already a few fairies and trolls along the river when we arrived. Hanging across the river were rows of flags in different colors. It looked so festive and exciting!

"This is so sweet!" Taffy said.

But then she pointed down the river and cried, "Over there! Cupcake and Swirlie are here."

I watched as Cupcake and Swirlie set out chairs and put on large sunglasses. "I guess all of Sugar Valley is here!" I exclaimed.

Frosting rolled his eyes. "Those are the biggest glasses I've ever seen. It looks like they want all of Sugar Valley to see *them*," he said.

Frosting looked around at all the boats. "Maybe next time *I* can ride with Gobo!"

I fluttered my wings. "Going fast was scary," I said. "But it was also kind of fun."

"There's your mom!" Taffy said. She pointed to the stage near the river. A castle

guard stood in front, holding a large red flag to start the race.

"Welcome, to the Choco-late River Race!" my mom announced.

"Let's start the first race of the day. This is one for beginner racers. Please move your boats to the starting line," she said.

There were loud cheers from the crowd along Chocolate River. I saw Gobo on his boat. I waved to him.

"His boat is **sugar-tastic**,"

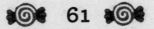

Frosting said. "I am definitely going to ask him for a ride after."

"Just check the weather first!" I said, smiling.

All boats were at the starting line. The guards lowered the red flags, and the race was on! **The boats zoomed down the river.** I could see Gobo **struggling** with his ropes, but he was in the lead! At the first turn, he had trouble with the sail, and he lost some time. The other boats were getting close!

"Go Gobo!" I called.

Taffy held up her sign, and Frosting flew up in the air pumping his fist.

Another troll on a green boat pulled ahead. And then a Candy Fairy in a rainbow boat sailed across the finish line!

Gobo came in third.

Taffy, Frosting, and I flew over to Gobo.

"That was a great first race!" Taffy said.

"I am sorry you didn't win,"

I said. "But you sailed really well."

Gobo didn't seem very happy. He tied his boat up and looked over at my mom. "Hello, Princess Lolli," he said.

She held out a trophy for Gobo. **"Congratulations, Gobo! You came in third place!"**

Gobo's whole face lit up. He held the chocolate trophy in his small hands.

"A trophy for third place?" he asked. "I really won a trophy?"

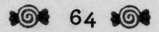

His parents and Toomie came
rushing over to him.
"Sure as sugar!" I
exclaimed, hugging Gobo.

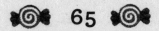

"I didn't even get a trophy for my first race," Toomie told him. He slapped Gobo on the back. **"Way to go!"**

His parents were grinning, and so was Gobo.

I was happy for my friend. We all were!

The Chocolate River Race was a chocolate challenge and a choco-late surprise!

Word List

combination (com·bih·NAY·shun): A mix

convince (kun·VINCE): To get someone to believe something

dismissal (dis·MISS·ull): Sending away

gripping (GRIP·ing): Having a firm hold

gust (GUHST): A strong blast of wind

mast (MAST): A long pole in a boat that holds the sail

similar (SIM·ih·lur): Almost the same

struggling (STRUG·ling): Making a hard and strong effort

swooshed (SWOOSHT): Moved quickly through the air

trophies (TRO·fees): Prizes or rewards

vanished (VAN·isht): Disappeared quickly

Questions

1. Why doesn't Gobo want to race?

2. What does Mini do when she is nervous?

3. Have you ever been on a boat?

4. What candy would you use to make a boat?

5. What was one of your favorite times with a new friend?

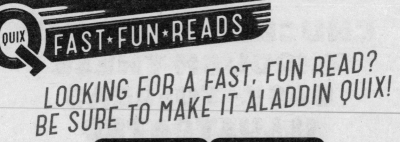

CHUCKLE YOUR WAY THROUGH THESE EASY-TO-READ ILLUSTRATED CHAPTER BOOKS!

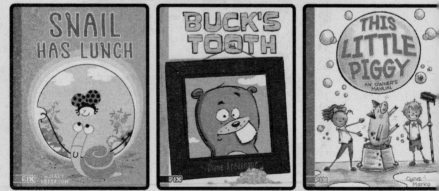